AMBER ARGYLE

OF FIRE AND ASH

D1453329

FAIRY QUEENS 3

This is a work of fiction. Names, characters, places, brands, media, and incidents are either the product of the author's imagination or are used fictitiously. The author acknowledges the trademarked status and trademark owners of various products, bands, and/or restaurants referenced in this work of fiction, which have been used without permission. The publication/use of these trademarks is not authorized, associated with, or sponsored by the trademark owners.

Copyright © 2015 by Amber Argyle
http://www.amberargyle.com

All rights reserved. Without limiting the rights under copyright reserved above, no part of this publication may be reproduced, stored in or introduced into a retrieval system, or transmitted, in any form, or by any means (electronic, mechanical, photocopying, recording, or otherwise) without the prior written permission of both the above copyright owner and the publisher of this book.

First Edition: January 2015
Library of Congress Cataloging-in-Publication Number: 2016909644

Argyle, Amber
Of Fire and Ash (Fairy Queens Series) – 1st ed
ISBN-13: 978-0-9976390-0-1

Visit Amber Argyle's website to sign up for her free starter library or to learn more: amberargyle.com

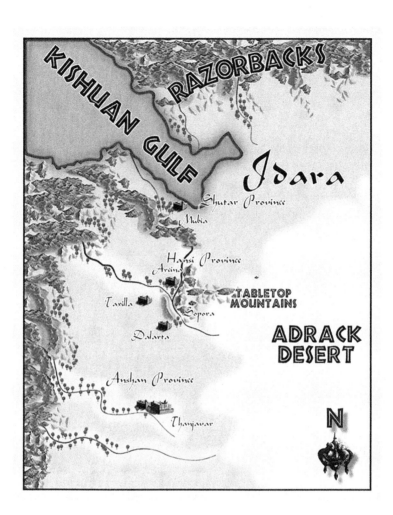

CHAPTER ONE

The blistering wind blowing in from the desert was so hot even the flies had disappeared. The only creatures still visible were the fairies Nelay had followed to the dry riverbed—fairies she was careful to never look at directly.

Sheep bleated impatiently around her as she pushed her handmade wooden shovel into the damp silt and dragged it back. She dug deeper and deeper. The sheep sniffed at the ground and crowded her. Her family's hobbled donkey even stepped on her foot. "Asat! Move!" She rammed him with her shoulder and shouted at the sheep. They scattered like oil in water, but it wasn't long before they turned to slowly circle Nelay, a circle that tightened with every turn.

Eventually, the dampness turned into mud, which gave way to puddles, the edges of which began to connect ever so slowly. Using her shovel, Nelay tossed clods of mud at the sheep. "Bossy! Patches! Get back!"

She managed to keep the animals off long enough to strain and drink her fill and replenish four water skins—two each for herself and her older brother, Panar. These she looped around her scrawny neck.

The water fairies flitted at the edge of her peripheral vision, but Nelay was practiced at avoiding them and didn't turn her head to watch.

Last, she unwound her headscarf and held it in the water, keeping it out of the mud as much as possible. When it was thoroughly soaked, she draped it back around her head and shoulders, her whole body relaxing in a silent sigh of relief.

As soon as she stood, the sheep charged the long fissure she'd created, nearly knocking her over as they sucked desperately at the water. She backed up, bumping and jostling against the two dozen sheep, the water skins banging against her ribs. Finally free of the animals, she flicked water off her fingers before hooking the shovel back on Asat's packsaddle.

She counted the sheep to make sure they were all there, starting with her favorites. Blua wore the bell. She was obedient, always the first to come when Nelay called. Her characteristic bleat—the *blua* sound that had inspired her name—was the loudest as she jostled with the others for access to the water.

Mag had a few blotches of black on her face that reminded Nelay of a magpie. Day was always the first one up in the mornings, and her mangled ear made her easy to find. And Farter . . . Nelay grinned.

All the sheep were accounted for except the one her father, Denar, had gone in search of. About a league from the water hole, he had noticed one of the pregnant ewes, Snotty, had gone missing. He'd told Nelay and Panar to go on ahead while he searched for her. Nelay bit her lip and tried not to think of the hours that had passed since her father left that morning.

Finished with her counting, she took two steps before bothering to look up and nearly collided with a bush. But what drew her up short wasn't the thorns—it was the fairy within the biting branches. Nelay stared at her wings, made of small leaves woven together with silk by spider mites. About the size of a small bird, the fairy was not beautiful as much as terrible. All the fairies were. For though they resembled mankind, with all the same features in the same places, their bodies were too thin, their faces too narrow. But even more than that was the bone-deep knowledge that Nelay was inferior.

For the fairies had magic.

Every night as long as Nelay could remember, her mother had whispered that Nelay must never acknowledge the fairies, with their beautiful wings and cruel faces. She must never let them realize she had the sight. Because if they knew, the priestesses of the Temple of Fire would come and take Nelay away.

And that was only if she survived the fairies' attention, for they were tricksy and cruel.

Nelay realized she'd been staring and forced her eyes to slide past the fairy, forced herself to continue past the bush as though she didn't feel shaken. She lifted one of the water skins to her mouth. The liquid tasted like dirt, the fine silt coating her tongue and sticking to her throat.

The banks of the dry riverbed were choked with dying brush. Watching for snakes, Nelay ignored another fairy as she climbed up the steep embankment. At the top, she had to grip her headscarf to keep the wind from snatching it off her head.

Her brother's sharp gaze searched the barren landscape, wide valleys between table mountains, so named for their steep, cliff-like sides and flat tops. With black hair, dark eyes, and dusky skin, Panar looked like a taller, angrier version of Nelay.

"Do you see him?" Nelay asked loudly to be heard over the wind.

"If I had, I would have told you by now." Panar said derisively. He was always mean when he was scared.

With only one sheep to slow her father down, Nelay had thought he would have caught up to them by now. "What are we going to do?"

Panar took his water skins from her and looped them over his neck and shoulder before taking a long drink. "Get down there and dig out that water hole again."

3

Nelay looked back. The sheep had trampled it, turning it into a muddy mess, which made it impossible for them to drink. It would probably need clearing out three or four times before they moved on.

"Why don't you dig it, and I'll watch?" she asked.

Panar shoved her. She stumbled, her foot landing half on and half off the embankment. Windmilling her arms, she barely managed to catch a brittle branch. It cracked, partially breaking off in her hand, but it was enough to steady her.

Only three years older than her, he thought twelve made him a man, and therefore in charge. She planted both fists on her hips and shot him a glare. "Rotten, maggoty sheep guts!" She had been saving that insult for just such a moment as this.

Panar whipped out his sling and filled it with a rock. Nelay took off, slipping and sliding down the dirt embankment to land on her knees on the dry riverbed. A rock thudded into the dirt beside her. He had missed.

Darting for cover behind the same bush the fairy hid inside, Nelay suppressed a fierce grin of satisfaction. She was a better shot—always had been. It goaded Panar, so he practiced every day, for hours.

Yet she was still better. Nelay knew better than to rub it in, though. He was bigger than her, and stronger, and any snide remarks would cost her dearly.

Another rock thwacked into the bush—if the poor plant wasn't already dead, Panar would probably kill it by day's end.

Trying very hard to ignore the fairy that was close enough to touch, Nelay waited until she was sure Panar had given up before she shuffled back to the water hole, which was worse than just muddy, as sheep didn't care much where they left their droppings. She sighed. That's why she always filled her family's water skins first.

Sheep weren't very smart. Her mother always said it was because they used all their energy to grow pretty wool. Nelay's

mother always took the opportunity to remind her that just because she had enormous brown eyes, a beautiful dusky complex-
ion, and hair that shone with a dark iridescence didn't mean she
should spend any energy thinking about it, or she'd wind up as
stupid as the sheep.

At the thought of her mother, Nelay felt guilt well up inside
her chest. Following the fairies to water was a dangerous thing to
do. She was bound to attract their attention if she kept it up.

But two years after the famine began, all the creeks had
dried up. If Nelay hadn't used her sight, her family would have
had to sell the sheep long ago.

At least the sheep weren't as desperately thirsty this time, so
they didn't crowd her as much as she cleared out the mud. She
backed up and let them have at it.

It wasn't long before they started to bed down in the shade.
After checking for snakes and scorpions in the protected spot
beside the bush the spider-mite fairy had hid inside, Nelay un-
loaded the tent from Asat's pack saddle. The *ovat*—ancient
Idaran for the dying wind—was almost upon them, and the tent
would provide protection from the intense heat.

She set up the tent same as she had a thousand times before.
Nelay didn't have any incense, but she reached into her pocket
and rubbed her thumb along the small glass idol her father had
bought her at the Arcina market last summer. Nelay's mother
had been angry when she'd seen the idol, an image of the Goddess of Fire, but she hadn't taken it away.

Nelay's thumb seemed to fit perfectly in the groove between the woman's folded wings. "Let the fire burn within me,"
Nelay muttered the invocation just as the low-level priestess had
showed her.

Finished with the tent, Nelay settled on her sheepskin rug
and dug in the pouch at her waist. On the walk here, she'd managed to find a few withered nuts and a couple of beetles, but it
wasn't more than a mouthful. She ate the beetles first so she

wouldn't be stuck with their aftertaste. She chewed the nuts slowly, making them last, but the meager amount only made her feel hungrier.

There had been a time when her family had had food. Not a lot of it, but enough. Such decadence seemed a lifetime ago.

Nelay remembered the last time it rained—a stingy sprinkle that had left concave indentations in the dirt. The world had smelled wonderful, of starving soil rejoicing in its first taste of water in months. But that had been all it was. A taste. Just enough to wet the soil's mouth and no more.

Panar slid down the embankment, sweat staining his robe, and his face flushed with heat even he couldn't endure for long. He started poking around at the base of the brush, no doubt trying to scare up a scorpion or, better yet, a lizard.

When he came up with nothing, he soaked his headscarf in the water, ate a handful of nuts, and lay down as far away from Nelay as he could get and still be in the tent. Within minutes, he was snoring.

A sudden burn of anger started in her chest. How could he sleep without hearing the scrape of Father's carving knife bringing dead wood to life? Without the smell of resin? Didn't Panar know that their father should have returned long ago—that something must be wrong?

Nelay rolled over, curling around her hollow stomach. She was hungry. She was always hungry. They all were. As the hours passed and still Father hadn't come, she grew more and more certain they couldn't go on like this—weaker and hungrier by the day.

If she could use her sight to track fairies and find water, surely she could use it to find something to eat. She could save them.

When the worst of the ovat had passed, Nelay slipped from the tent. Panar could watch the sheep. He could dig out the hole.

She moved quietly to their donkey, Asat, and pulled her spear out of the packsaddle. Nelay made sure her brother was still sleeping, then tied her headscarf over her face to protect it from the wind and started out.

Even at the base of the riverbed, the hardiest of plants were brittle with death. Every day, Nelay and her father and brother had to range farther and farther to find anything for the sheep to forage. As she moved away from the water, the plant fairies grew scarce. It wasn't like each bush had its own fairy. More like one fairy oversaw each species of plant within its territory.

A person without the sight would see only an insect, a mouse, a bird, or sometimes nothing at all. But Nelay saw a mouse fairy, with whiskers and twitchy ears, hovering over a warren. She could only guess at the creature's purpose. At any rate, a mouse would only be a mouthful, so she moved on.

There were lots of spider fairies, with eight creepy eyes stacked on top of each other, a furry dress, and spider silk wings. But Nelay was sick of eating bugs. She wanted meat.

As the wind slacked off, a nervous flutter started in her belly. If her brother hadn't awakened already, he would soon. They were never supposed to leave the sheep—or each other. She and Panar were supposed to protect the sheep from lions and jackals, but the last time Nelay had seen a predator more dangerous than a lone leopard was when a pride had attacked the flock over a year ago and killed all their sheep dogs.

Since then, even the jackals had abandoned this place. There was nothing worth staying for.

Nelay caught sight of a few more plant fairies out of the corner of her eye. She was careful never to lock gazes with them, for then they would know she could see them.

She paused when she spotted a fairy darting back and forth above a large, bleached branch, her wings shining with scales. Nelay stepped closer and saw the subtle pattern in the fairy's wings—the same pattern as a spitting cobra.

A swift spike of fear burned through her veins. All her life, she'd avoided snakes, for every single one was poisonous. Some just killed faster than others. The big cobras could spit more than twice as far as Nelay was tall. But she doubted she'd find anything else. And if she came back empty-handed, Panar would make sure he didn't miss with his stones.

Hooking her spear on her belt, Nelay reached into her second pouch, feeling the smooth stones she was always on the lookout for. She chose one without actually glancing at it—she could tell by the feel that it was perfect.

She pulled her sling from her belt and settled the stone in the cup. The fairy had stopped her frantic flying and was hovering, watching. But Nelay couldn't think of the fairy, or the fact that she'd attracted her attention. Not taking her eyes from the branch, Nelay bent down and grabbed a large stick, worn smooth by the dead river and made brittle by the heat. She tossed it at the large branch and heard a hiss in response.

Keeping her eyelids slitted just in case, she threw another. Another hiss and then a long snake the size of her arm rose up, its hood flared at the sides of its delicate head. It was black, except for the nearly translucent skin below the hood, which was covered in a greasy-looking substance the color of rotted sheep's milk. The snake was shedding its skin.

Without hesitation Nelay wound up once and let the rock fly. And missed.

The cobra reared back and spit, its poison striking her legs. With a backward stumble, she swallowed her yelp. The snake slithered over the rock in a blur of sinuous movement, coming at her.

Nelay didn't have time to think. She ran. Being hungry was better than dying from snake venom. When she dared look back, the snake still chased her but was far enough back to be out of spitting range. Gulping a deep breath, she filled her sling, spun around, and let it fly.

When the snake jerked, Nelay knew she'd hit it. It spit at her, but this time the poison landed in the dirt before her. She wound up and released another rock. The creature flopped down and went still.

She gaped in disbelief. She'd killed it. Something so scary and deadly, and she, a nine-year-old girl, had killed it. A grin spread across Nelay's face, but slid off when she felt the snake fairy's watchful gaze.

Taking her spear from her belt, Nelay approached the snake cautiously. Its head was smashed and oozing blood. Panar said they could still bite even after they were dead. She didn't know if that was true or not, but she wasn't taking any chances. She dropped a huge rock on the creature's head and sawed it off with her spear, leaving the head under the rock.

Every instinct in her screamed against reaching out and grabbing its tail, but there was no other way to bring the meat home. As soon as she touched it, the body writhed and the stump struck her arm. With a scream, Nelay dropped it and stumbled back, her heart leaping in her chest.

She snatched a handful of river silt and scrubbed the blood and fluids from her skin. When she looked up, the snake fairy hovered nearby, watching her.

Nelay pressed her wrists to her temples and pinched her eyes shut. She'd done the one thing her mother had warned her never to do—she'd captured the fairy's attention. Terror pumped through Nelay's body as the headless snake continued to writhe. And then she swallowed her fear. She'd ignore the fairy, as she always did. It was bound to lose interest in her eventually.

As for the snake, she'd seen other creatures do this after they'd died—thrash as if their bodies didn't accept their death. Still, she couldn't bring herself to touch it again.

Shaking, she stabbed the snake with her spear and lifted it up, carrying it as far away from her body as she could manage. It was huge, twice as long as she was tall. But pretty soon, her arms tired and she gave up on fear and instincts and just draped it over her shoulder, where the shedding skin moved weirdly against her and the greasy substance stained her threadbare robes.

But even worse than the snake trying to curl around her was the incessant flap of the fairy's wings. It was following her.

Nelay hadn't gone far when she heard Panar calling for her. She didn't want to answer—he would be angry. But not answering would only make it worse. "I'm here."

He came running into view, his spear in hand and his headscarf wrapped around his face. Never breaking his stride, his eyes went over her from head to toe. "Where have you been? Father told us never to leave the sheep!"

"You left them," she shot back.

Jerking back his headscarf, he stopped in front of her, sweat running down the sides of his face. She held the snake between them in an attempt to distract him. His gaze caught greedily on the meat and he took it from her without question, slinging it over his own shoulder. Then he grasped her upper arm and dragged her toward the waterhole. "How did you get this?"

Nelay tried to pull away. "I killed it."

His head whipped around. "With what?"

His fingers dug painfully in her arm, and she tried to pry his hand off. "With my sling."

A muscle in his jaw ticked. "That's impossible."

Anger flared in Nelay. "Just because you couldn't make that shot doesn't mean I can't."

He stopped, shame and jealousy flashing across his eyes in turn. "You think you're better than me?"

It would have been smart to deny it, back down. But Nelay had risked her life so they'd have something to eat, and all he could worry about was his pride. "I know I'm better than you."

He shoved her and she stumbled back. Before she could catch herself, he was on top of her, the snake's body pinned between them. "Who do you think is going to get it when Father finds out I let you hunt a cobra?"

She dug her heels into the dirt, trying to scramble out from under him. But he was too big. "One of us had to." She shot out, meaning to hurt him.

It worked. His hands clamped around her throat. "I hate you," he said, his eyes clouded with fury. "Someday I'm going to get out of this cursed desert. I'm going to be an important man. And you're going to be married and pregnant. That's all you'll ever be. The only future you'll ever have. You understand me?"

Like acid, black spots ate holes in Nelay's vision. Her mouth worked, trying to scream at him to let go, to let her have air, but his hands were too tight. She squirmed, clawing at his fingers. He shook her as if that would force an answer out of her.

So she spit in his face. She knew it was a bad idea, but he deserved it.

His gaze narrowed and he squeezed harder, so hard her vision went dark and her muscles went soft. And then everything turned black.

When she came to, Panar was gone and so was the snake. The ground felt hot beneath her, so hot it almost burned her, which meant she hadn't been lying there long. Her ears rang. She sat up and gingerly touched her neck, feeling the welts where her brother's fingers had been. She couldn't see, but she knew bruises stained her skin. Tears blurred her vision, so she squeezed her eyes shut and forced the tears down.

Her brother's words rang in her memory, chafing more than the pain in her neck. She thought of her mother, pregnant with her sixth child. Bulging veins ran through her legs like swollen rivers, the skin of her abdomen torn in vertical lines. She thought of her mother weeping over three gray babies so small they fit in the palm of Nelay's hand. Blood and tears—that was the lot of women.

Was it the only future for her?

She pushed herself up on shaky arms and locked gazes with the snake fairy. She made herself look away, but not before she noticed the fairy's slitted tongue flick out of its mouth. "Burn it, bird, stop following me," she muttered, hoping the fairy would buy the lie.

Nelay wrapped her headscarf around her head and neck, then staggered back up the dry riverbed. When she reached the water hole, she found it had been dug out again. Panar was blowing on a nest of smoking, shredded bark, his flint and knife beside his knees. He didn't glance up at her. She glared at him for good measure before discreetly scanning the area for the viper fairy. Not seeing it, she sagged in relief and slipped inside the tent to lie down.

When she woke, it was because her mouth watered. She wiped the drool from her cheek and sat up. Smelling meat, she stepped outside, relieved when she still didn't see the snake fairy. It must have lost interest in her. The worst of the day's heat had passed, which meant the ovat was over. The fairy was nowhere to be seen. Nelay let out a sigh of relief and counted the sheep, most of which now grazed.

Panar had gutted the snake and strung it above the fire. Its dark skin hung over a branch, drying. Her brother was already eating.

Without a word, Nelay took her knife from her belt and cut from the top, hissing through her teeth as the meat burned her fingers. She bounced a piece on her palm and dropped it on a flat rock that had been scrubbed clean. That, along with the freshly dug water hole and dinner, was Panar's way of saying sorry.

Nelay ignored him, her way of saying he wasn't forgiven. He was older and a boy. He expected to be better at everything. So every time her father praised her for finding a water hole, or hitting a target with her sling, or doing what she was told, Panar took it as a personal insult. And she was sick of it.

She cut off pieces of meat, set them on the rock to cool a bit, and popped them into her mouth. Snake wasn't bad. She'd certainly had worse—the beetles at midday, for example, were terrible—but she didn't like the way the reptile's bones stuck going down her throat.

She and Panar ate without saying a word. Nelay ate until she knew she'd be sick if she took one more bite. Swallowing to keep her gorge down, she gave voice to the worry lurking silent and heavy just beyond sight. "Father isn't back yet." Her voice was gravelly, and it hurt to talk.

Panar smacked his lips as he sucked the grease off his fingers. "I know."

"What are we going to do?"

He cut more of the meat off the stick, then set it on his rock to cool. "I'm going to go look for him."

Nelay still refused to look at her brother. "I'm coming too." They had another six hours of daylight.

"No. You stay with the sheep. There's enough grazing for one more day. I'll bring him back."

Nelay wanted to protest, but her neck was still sore, and Panar was right. "When are you going?"

He stuffed the cooled meat into his food pouch. "Now." He picked up his spear and climbed the embankment. Within seconds, he was out of sight.

And Nelay was alone.

CHAPTER TWO

Morning came with no sign of Panar or their father. Nelay watched the cold blue sky go from charcoal to pale blue. She glanced around the clearing—no fairies in sight. There usually weren't after she lit a fire. They didn't seem to like smoke.

She hadn't had time to properly cure the meat—that took days—but she had done the best she could over the long, cold night. She rose to her feet, her sheepskin draped around her shoulders. Obviously, something was wrong. Her brother and father must be hurt or lost.

Nelay took down their tent, then dug out the water hole until she stood in ankle-deep water. She drank as much water as her stomach could hold, wet her headscarf, and refilled her water skins.

After tying the packsaddle onto Asat, she started off. But the sounds of a discordant bell made her turn. Blua, their lead sheep, was following Nelay, as she always did, making her trademark bleat. And where Blua went, the other sheep followed.

Nelay tied Asat to a bush, which the donkey immediately started nibbling, Nelay took hold of Blua's collar and led her back to the water hole.

She ran her hands over the sheep's ears, popping off any ticks she found, then rubbed the sheep's head. Blua leaned into the touch, moving her head in time with Nelay's scratches. Emotions rose in Nelay's throat, but she held them off before they overwhelmed her. Using a string, she tied Blua so she could still reach the water. Then Nelay quickly walked back to Asat, tears burning her eyes.

Refusing to look back as Blua bleated at her, Nelay walked along the embankment until she found a place Asat could manage. The donkey followed her up and over. Almost immediately, Nelay felt like she was being watched. But she could see no one.

It wasn't hard to find the tracks from the day before—there were broken branches and fresh mounds of pebbly sheep dung everywhere, her brother's fresher prints superimposed over the older ones. But yesterday they'd taken a wandering route, following what little feed they could find. Now, Nelay cut straight through. And still she sensed someone was there, staring, following her, but every time she turned, there was nothing but dirt and dry shrubs.

Along the way, she saw four fairies. A hawk fairy with a sharp, yellow beak and feathered wings. A lizard fairy with horns growing from her back. A scorpion fairy with a poisonous barb on her sectioned tail. The forth was another spider fairy.

Nelay was drenched in sweat and dizzy by the time the ovat started. She wanted to simply drink her second water skin and press on—she wasn't that far from where her father had broken away—but that would be foolish, the kind of foolish that could get her killed.

There were rules to surviving the desert. One water skin before the ovat break, one after. Drink as much as you can at each water hole. Never stop looking for food. Always keep your sling within reach and your spear nearby. Don't ever run from lions or hyenas.

With a growl of frustration, Nelay hobbled Asat so he could find something to eat. She checked for venomous critters before settling down in the shade of a creosote bush. She let the last drops from her first water skin trickle down her cracked throat, careful not to let one drop spill.

After rubbing her glass idol and whispering the invocation, she ate some of the cold snake meat—if possible it was even stringier and tougher than the day before. Nelay rubbed the grease on her chapped lips and lay down. Though she was exhausted, she couldn't sleep for the worry pressing against her. After about two hours, the ovat passed, so she rounded up Asat, allowed herself another mouthful of water to soothe her aching throat, and started out again.

Finally, she found where she and Panar had separated from their father not long after Snotty went missing. Nelay tied up Asat, then pulled herself up one of the steep sides of the tabletop mountain. She placed her feet with care, for snakes liked the shade under the rocks this time of day. When she'd gone high enough to see all of the low valley, she shaded her eyes and spied a thin line of smoke to the west, next to the table mountain. Her father and brother were the only people out here, so the sign of fire meant they were that way. After a full day without water, her father would be heat sick.

Nelay hadn't seen any water fairies, or the types of fairies only found around water, such as moss fairies or butterfly fairies. She scanned the area, searching for any tell-tale signs of green that might indicate water. Seeing nothing, she realized the nearest water hole was the one she'd left that morning. Nearly a full day's journey away.

Forcing down the foreboding rising inside her, she traced out some of the landmarks, making a mental map in her head, and trotted down the hill. It wasn't terribly far to where the smoke came from, so picked up her pace. When she finally got close enough to smell the fire, she called out, "Father? Panar?"

"Nelay!" Her brother answered, his voice cracking with emotion.

She ran halfway up the rise leading to the mountain before she remembered to watch for snakes and forced herself to slow down. She pushed through some brush and could finally see her father. He was propped against the steep mountain face, his face ashen and part of his robe missing.

Her gaze immediately went to his foot, which was bound in strips of cloth. A tourniquet gripped his thigh. Her mother would be angry that he'd damaged the robe she'd woven by hand.

Shaking her head, Nelay dismissed the stray thought. "What happened?" she panted as she knelt opposite of Panar.

"A snake bit him," her brother choked out.

Nelay noted the swelling through the bandage. There was dried blood on the ground. She followed it to see another dead snake cooking over the fire—even in such frightening times as this, they did not waste food.

Her gaze went to the snake skin, laid flat over some of the rocks.

It was a black mamba.

"No!" she gasped, her head feeling light and heavy at once. Mamba bites were always, always deadly. Her wide gaze shifted to Panar.

He was crying hard now, snot and tears running down his face. Nelay ground her teeth to bit back the bitter words she wanted to say. She hated him for crying. It wasn't fair that he could break down, but she had to be the strong one. And afterward, he would only hate her for it. "You're wasting water," she ground out.

Her father's rough finger scraped across the top of her hand. "Water."

She gave him her water skin. He drank all of it, and Nelay knew how bad it was. Her father was unwavering in his water preservation.

"Why didn't you come get me?" Nelay directed her question at Panar.

He wiped his nose on his sleeve. "I couldn't leave him."

Their father was twice Panar's size. There was no way he could have carried him. "You should have! You needed Asat!"

"Stop arguing," her father said, his voice so low she could barely hear him.

Nelay felt a hot wash of shame. "Did you ever find Snotty?"

"No," her father replied, and Nelay's chest hurt. "Where are the sheep?"

"I left them at the watering hole," she said.

Her father nodded, patting her arm with his hand. "Good girl. I knew you'd have the sense to leave them and bring Asat. It's why I didn't send your brother after you."

His praise made Nelay feel bigger, but she knew she would pay for her father's implied dig at Panar.

Panar pushed to his feet and stomped to the fire to turn the snake.

Nelay braced herself and unwound the wrapping over her father's foot. There were two perfect puncture marks, dimpled in skin swollen so tight it was shiny. From his toes to the middle of his shin, the flesh was an angry purple. "What do we do, Father?"

After a moment, he took a deep breath and looked at her. "It should have killed me within an hour. But it didn't. You have to get me to your mother. She'll know what to do."

Nelay calculated their circuitous route in her head. "But that will take two weeks, at least."

Her father pointed to the north. "Not if we cut straight through."

Nelay followed his gesture, where their home lay two days' walk away. "But we never go that way—there's no water." Not a river, not a spring, nothing. She pointed back to the southeast, where she'd come from. "But I found water in the dried-up creek, a day in that direction."

"Nelay, if anyone can find water, you can." Her father's eyes shone with pride, and she noticed Panar's fists tightening with anger.

He hated her for being better. He didn't know she wasn't better because of any superior skill but because of her sight. And she couldn't tell him. "I can't find it if it isn't there," Nelay said in a small voice.

Father shook his head. "We have to get to your mother before my leg dies—if it does, I'll die with it."

Nelay saw the fear in his eyes. But even at the age of nine, she recognized that little of that fear was for himself. She and Panar couldn't care for the sheep alone. How would they survive if Father died?

She stared toward home, wishing there was a way to skip across the mountaintops—like she could gather her father in her arms and jump. Ten, maybe eleven jumps and they'd be home. Panar could walk.

She sighed. There would be no jumping. If they traveled all night, they'd lose less water. They would be heat sick, but they would survive. There was no choice. They had to go. "What about the sheep?" she asked. Without their the coins from selling their wool, the family wouldn't survive long. But it was more than that. The sheep were her friends—the only ones she had. It would be five days before they could come back for them. If the sheep muddied up the waterhole, they'd die of thirst before then. And that was if a wild beast didn't kill them first.

Panar knelt again but refused to look at Nelay or their father. "I'll go back and tend them."

"Your sister can't do this by herself."

"She can do everything else by herself," Panar mumbled.

Nelay felt the bruises on her neck, anger pricking her heart. She considered telling her father how Panar had choked her. But if she held the knowledge close, she could use it against her brother when she really needed it. Besides, she wanted to watch him squirm.

Father shot Panar a sharp look. "And who's going to help her lift me onto Asat after I pass out?"

Panar's mouth opened, then closed again.

"You're going to pass out?" Nelay asked.

Her father's over-bright eyes fixed on her. "Daughter, I'll be lucky to make it all the way home."

Swallowing hard, she met Panar's gaze and saw the fear there. "I'll prepare Asat. You get the meat."

She pulled the packsaddle off the donkey, revealing a dark, rectangular stain of sweat on his back. To try to protect the saddle from the elements, she stashed it under a bush. She left the tent, cooking implements, and other odds and ends, but took the blankets and put a few items in her pockets. Then she set aside her spear to take with her.

Panar had already brought their father some meat, which he ate slowly. Nelay and Panar took hold of his arms and hauled him to his feet while he hissed in pain. Somehow, they heaved him partway onto the donkey's back. The animal shifted and brayed in protest—he wasn't used to being ridden, and Father was heavier and larger than Asat's regular load.

The donkey lurched to the side, which nearly caused Father to slip off. Nelay grabbed his leg and locked her knees, bracing herself while Panar steadied Asat. Finally, Father was able to swing his other leg over the animal's back. After nothing bad happened, Asat settled down. Father lay down on the donkey's neck, his arms dangling past the beast's shoulders.

Nelay glanced at the sky. They had a few hours to full dark. "We'll tack northeast until this mountain flattens out. I'll scout ahead for water."

Her father spoke with his eyes closed. "Be careful." His voice was tight with pain. "We can't risk having anyone else bitten."

She nodded, then draped her empty water skins around her neck and took her spear in one hand. "I will, Father." She grabbed a few strips of meat out of her pouch to give her strength for the long march, wishing for a sip of water to wash it down her already-dry throat.

After she took several long strides, she glanced back at Panar and saw the pleading in his face. For all that he pretended he was a man, he wasn't yet. "Go slow," she said, angry that he always expected her to fix things.

Panar nodded, and she turned from them. Using her spear as a walking stick, she moved at a steady pace through the brush, her every sense attuned to the rhythm and flow of the desert. There were small signs of food, but she ignored them, instead searching for water fairies.

For anyone without the sight, the desert appeared a desolate place. But it was never as desolate as it seemed. The animals were simply hiding, deep in the ground or tucked in the crags of rocks or beneath dying bushes. After nightfall, when the shadows robbed mankind of vision, those creatures emerged and roamed through the cool dark.

The fairies were even better hidden. Some people saw a bird, a bug, or nothing at all, their eyes passing over the fairies without actually seeing them. But the fairies weren't hidden from Nelay. She scoured the landscape for a moss fairy, a water fairy, for fairies whose animals made their lairs by water—leopards, sand cats, hyenas. Her desperation increased as she found nothing.

The dusky turquoise sky gave no sign of the sun's existence besides a smudged, pale-blue print in the distance. Nelay moved to a trot—it would waste her body's water reserves, but if she didn't find anything before dark, she'd have to wait for morning.

She caught sight of a leather wing and whipped around, her heart pounding. Was the fairy still following her after all? But she saw nothing. Steeling herself, she pressed on, searching. She finally stopped when it was too dark to see. There was no water. Hope had kept her moving. And now that hope was gone.

Legs aching, she trudged to the side of the steep, cliff-like slope of another tabletop mountain and slumped down to light a smoky fire so Panar could find her. She drew her knees to her chest, her head throbbing and her mouth and eyes swollen. Her whole body screamed silently for water.

Was her father even still alive? She reached into her pocket and withdrew the glass idol. Her thumbs worked up the slippery wings as she mouthed the words over and over. "Let the fire burn within me."

She awoke sometime later to Panar kicking her legs. She sat up with a start to find him standing above her, holding the donkey's lead rope. "Where's the water?"

Working her swollen tongue to try to bring up some moisture in her mouth, Nelay pushed herself to her feet. She staggered with sudden dizziness and rubbed at the cramp in her leg. "There isn't any."

The fire reflecting off his face, Panar shot a worried look back at their father. "Sister, we have to have water!"

"I can't find what isn't there!" She studied her father, draped over their donkey, his face screwed up in pain, his breathing labored. She glanced quickly away. "I won't be able to find anything in the dark, Father."

He didn't answer.

She shot Panar a panicked look. Her brother swallowed hard. "He keeps falling asleep," he said. "It's hard to wake him."

Nelay strode to her father and shook his shoulder. His head turned away from her touch. Squeezing, she shook him. His eyes opened.

She stepped back. "I couldn't find any water."

Her father grunted something incoherent and rested his head against the donkey once more.

Nelay bit her knuckle as she stared at him, aghast.

"He's going to be fine," Panar said stubbornly.

She nodded a little too emphatically. It would be a quarter moon, just enough light to see by. "If we have the valley crossed by morning, we can reach Mother by this time tomorrow."

Nelay started out. Panar jerked on the donkey's lead rope and followed.

CHAPTER THREE

With air sawing in and out of her lungs, Nelay finally reached the top of a table mountain. Sweat should be pouring down her, yet it wasn't. She would have been frightened, but it was getting harder and harder to worry about anything except her next step. And the next step after that.

She knew she was being watched, but she was very careful not to look for the snake fairy now. Her only hope was that the creature would lose interest and go away.

Leaning against her spear, Nelay looked back. Panar staggered up the rise toward her, the donkey trailing behind him. The animal's ears drooped tiredly. He had started to stumble more and more. How much longer before he flopped down and refused to rise? How much longer before all of them flopped down and refused to rise?

But if they pushed through, they could be home by tonight. Mother would have goats milk and cheese and cooked grains, and cool water from their well.

Nelay turned her face toward the hot breeze that whipped her headscarf free and twisted her robes against her ankles. Tugging the headscarf back over her face and holding it, she started across the flat expanse with a quicker step. When she finally reached the other side, she searched the landscape below, looking for any signs of water, water fairies, or the snake fairy still following her. There was nothing.

Ignoring her persistent headache, Nelay searched for a suitable place to descend. To the south, a fan of land spanned out. She whistled to catch Panar's attention and pointed so he could head straight for it. Then she made her way across the top of the mountain and down the other side, sliding on her bottom when it grew too steep.

At the base, she sank to the ground, her head pounding and her heart thudding painfully in her chest, and watched as Panar and the donkey picked their way down. Sometime in the night, her father had slipped off the animal's back. He had awakened enough to help them get him back on. After that, they'd tied him around the animal's neck.

Suddenly, the donkey stumbled and lurched forward. With a shout, Panar jumped out of the way. Before Nelay could process what had happened, the donkey flipped, sending her father flying through the air. He hit hard and skidded down the slope. Nelay started running, the donkey's brays sounding far away.

Panar reached Father first. Nelay skidded to a stop beside them, dust sticking to her throat and making her cough. "Father?"

He reached toward his wound, his whole body clenched in pain. "My leg."

Nelay exchanged a look with Panar before pulling the bandage back. A large chunk of her father's skin about the size of her hand came with it. Blood oozed from the wound, which was surrounded by unnaturally white flesh. Nelay didn't have a drop of water to wash the blood away.

Gagging, Panar stood and backed away. His head swiveled from side to side. "Where's Asat?"

Nelay staggered to her feet. "Asat!" she called. They jumped up and searched frantically, but the donkey was gone.

Breathing hard, Nelay sat back down, her forearms resting on her drawn knees. "Father, Asat is gone."

He let out a few hard breaths and opened his eyes. His eyes were bloodshot and bulging. He glanced at his leg and grimaced. "Listen to me now. Both of you, go on home. Fetch Benvi and his sons. Have them come for me." Benvi was their closest neighbor, a half day's walk away.

Nelay shook her head so hard her headscarf came loose and pooled around her shoulders. "By the time we get him, we won't be able to come back here until tomorrow before the ovat." She knew her father wouldn't survive that long without water.

Panar was still and silent on the other side of their father. "We can't leave him," she pleaded with her brother.

When Panar didn't respond, she felt a sob heaving in her throat. She had to make them understand. "If we leave him, he'll die."

Panar finally raised his eyes to hers. "That's why he's sending us away. So we don't die with him."

A sob burst from Nelay's throat. Crying without producing tears made her headache blaze. "No! You go. I'll stay here and find water. You come back with the others."

"Daughter," Father said softly. She refused to look at him. He rested his hand gently on her arm. "It'll be all right. Go with your brother. He'll care for you."

She finally met her father's gaze. "No."

"Nelay, listen to me! If you don't find water soon, you will die."

"So you want us to leave you to die!"

Her father reached up and took her shaking body in his arms. She collapsed against his chest, feeling the fever burning through him, and sobbed until her head felt like it would burst.

When she'd finally calmed herself, hard pulses of pain shot around her eyes. Father rubbed her back, something he'd never done before. "Drag me into the shade. Leave me with a spear and a knife."

So that he could fight off any predators that smelled the blood. Something hardened within Nelay. She would not lose her father. Not when she could stop it. "Father, there might be water. I saw something up on the mountain." A lie. She had formed another plan—one that had nothing to do with finding water. "I might have to dig for hours, but I can get some."

Father seemed to consider. "If you're wrong, it will be too late. Go with your brother." He held out his arms for them to take. "Help me."

She and Panar each hooked an arm around his elbow and dragged him over to a bush. "Not this one, Father," Nelay said with a nod toward the spines.

"That's why I chose it," he said breathlessly.

Suddenly she understood. The spines would protect him from wild beasts.

Panar swept his spear under the spiny branches. Nelay hoped he would flush something out—even a scorpion would provide them some moisture, but there was nothing.

Her brother stuck the butt of the spear into the bush and pushed up the branches. Father lay on his back and, with Nelay's help, managed to slide under. Then Panar gently lowered the branches.

Father spoke to them, his face obscured by thorns. "My children, I will fight to live with all I have, if you will promise the same."

"Yes, Father," Panar said, his gaze fastened to the ground.

Nelay could only nod.

Father took a deep breath and let it out slowly. "Go now."

Panar gave a hard jerk of his head for Nelay to follow, passed his spear to his other hand, and started out.

She trailed after him, looking back at the bush until it had disappeared from sight. When she was sure they were out of Father's earshot, she reached forward and took hold of her brother's sleeve. "Panar?"

He cocked his head back but didn't stop moving. "What?"

"I meant what I said. I can find water."

"Father said no."

She stumbled on a bump in the ground and fell to her knees. She didn't bother standing back up. "If I don't bring him water, he'll die."

Panar's shoulders slumped, and he finally stopped walking, though he didn't turn to face her. "He's going to die anyway, Nelay. His skin is starting to rot. Maybe it's better this way."

Nelay's whole body went numb. "How is it better if he dies?"

Panar whirled on her. "The only way to save him from the poison is to cut off his foot, but then he'll bleed to death. Better for him to die whole." His voice hitched. "There's nothing we can do."

"You don't know that," she said in a whisper.

He looked away, jiggling his spear. "You're coming with me, Nelay."

Pushing herself unsteadily to her feet, she backed out of his range, dropped her spear, and pulled her sling from her belt. She had it loaded with a stone in seconds.

Her brother reached for his own sling. "Nelay," he said, warning in his voice.

"You can't make me go."

"Just for once, follow *me*." He pounded his chest for emphasis, his eyes begging her.

Though she was only nine, Nelay knew he was asking for more than simple obedience. If she went against him now, he'd never forgive her. And even after everything he'd done to her, she didn't want that. "I can't."

He jerked out his own sling. Before he could even load a stone, she flung hers, letting go on the second rotation. Her stone flew perfectly, hitting his hand.

Panar hissed in pain, clutching his hand and shooting her a murderous glare. She filled her sling with another stone but kept backing away. "I can save him. You have to believe me."

He started toward her. She twisted her sling again, this time hitting his shoulder.

With a cry, he staggered back. Nelay knew he'd have a massive bruise. But she wouldn't back down. "Go!"

He charged toward her, but she flung another stone, hitting his chest.

"Fine," he spat, his eyes rimmed red with fury. "Stay and die."

He whirled around and stormed away. Nelay watched him go, her resolve suddenly wavering. She was terrified to be left alone. Terrified that her perfect plan didn't seem so perfect anymore. And even though what she was about to do would surely cost her freedom, maybe even her life, it was all she had.

She waited until she couldn't see or hear her brother before retrieving her spear and taking a defensive stance. Then she said softly, "You've been following me."

There was only stillness, and a shard of doubt pierced her heart. It wasn't too late to catch up to her brother, if he didn't throttle her beyond her ability to walk.

Steeling herself, she turned in a slow circle, searching every branch and shadow. It was time to break every rule her mother had taught her. "I saw you . . . you were helping that snake shed its skin, weren't you?"

Still nothing.

"My mother says I must never let the fairies know I can see them. She says, 'When gods and mankind mix, mankind always loses.' But you're a snake fairy. And snakes have venom. Maybe your magic can stop the venom."

"And what makes you think I would help you, mortal child?" a voice hissed.

Nelay nearly jumped out of her skin. She whirled around to find the fairy flying in a sinuous, snakelike pattern toward her. Allowing herself to look, Nelay saw things she'd never noticed before. The ropes of the fairy's inky hair were gathered at the top of her head before hanging halfway down her back. Her large ears pointed away from her head. Black markings lined her eyes and trailed in points down her cheeks. Her lips were blood-red, her fangs visible even when her mouth was closed. Scales covered her wings and most of her body, with lighter bands across her chest that gradually came to a point somewhere above her knees. Cloth hung from her body, fluttering as she moved. Either her feet were pointed or she wore pointed shoes. And her fingers ended in black claws.

Nelay shuddered but managed to hold her ground.

"I have no love for your kind—I am the keeper of snakes," the fairy announced.

Nelay fumbled for some kind of response. Honestly, she hadn't thought past simply asking for help—something even the meanest of humans wouldn't have withheld. But this wasn't a human. Nelay must remember that. "You were following me—there has to be something you want."

The snake fairy's tongue flicked out, tasting the air, and a shiver crawled down Nelay's spine. "The air is heavy with your fear."

Nelay wished her mind wasn't so thick with thirst. "My mother does that when she doesn't want to answer my father—says something to distract him."

The fairy smiled, revealing a black mouth. "Clever, aren't you?"

A touch of anger made Nelay puff her chest out. "What's your name?"

The wings stiffened. "Siseth," the fairy finally said.

Nelay let out a bit of the breath she'd been holding. "There's something you want, Siseth. Something that can be bargained for."

Siseth eased down to crouch on a rock, her wings curling around her. "Bargained? No. Something to be taken."

The threat rolled off the fairy as her body coiled to strike. Nelay's fingers inched toward the pouch of rocks at her waist.

Siseth tracked her movements. "You think you can hurt me? I am immortal."

Nelay swallowed. "I can try."

Siseth darted forward so fast that Nelay stumbled back. She brought her spear up, instinctively swiping at the creature. She felt a tiny shudder as the spear connected. Siseth fell, landing in a broken heap.

Nelay blinked in disbelief, easing forward. It felt ridiculous to rest a spear tip against the tiny fairy's chest, but she did it anyway. She pushed gently, but Siseth didn't move. Unable to resist, Nelay reached out and brushed her fingers against the scaly, bat-like wings.

The fairy was dead. How was that possible? She'd claimed immortality. And now Nelay had killed her only chance at saving her father. She dropped to her knees and cradled her head in her hands.

CHAPTER FOUR

A sudden slither and rush of movement brought Nelay's head up and her spear around, but too slowly to stop the cobra from clamping onto her hand with the force of a hammer.

She screamed and brought her spear around to swing at the snake, but as quickly as it had struck, the cobra shot away. Nelay dropped her spear and cradled her throbbing hand to her chest, staring at the twin puncture wounds.

She collapsed, defeat and fear and hopelessness washing over her. She looked up to see the snake watching her from just out of reach, its tongue flicking in and out. Nelay picked up her spear with her left hand and growled, "You sack of stringy meat, come get me."

The snake rose up, its hood flaring and growing wider and wider before Nelay's eyes. Gasping, she stumbled back. The hood split in two, spreading to the side of its head before fanning into wings. The body shortened, while the tail split into legs. The snake's pointed head flattened and lightened, hair sprouting in thick coils. Cloth fluttered from a dress made of scales. Within seconds, the snake had transformed into Siseth.

Nelay stared at the fairy's broken body—there were two of them now. One dead, one alive. A hysterical giggle bubbled up in her throat. She swallowed it down. "How . . ."

"I said I was immortal, not that I couldn't be killed," Siseth replied, the haughtiness gone from her tone. She flew closer, but more slowly this time.

With a deep throb, Nelay remembered the burning pain in her hand. The snake bite was just to the side of the valley between her thumb and finger. Her eyes grew heavy and her lungs felt tight—she couldn't seem to draw a breath. "Am I going to die?"

The fairy was even closer now, staring at Nelay's wound in apparent fascination. "It would take much more than one bite to kill you."

Nelay hefted her spear. "Are you trying to scare me?"

The fairy darted. Nelay tried to swat at it again, but she was too slow. She only had time to see it crouching on her hand, the tiny, clawed fingers spearing her wound before pain blazed up her arm.

Nelay screamed and everything went white.

She came to on the ground, bits of gravel embedded into abrasions on her cheek. She must have scraped it when she collapsed.

She glanced at her hand. Gasping, she saw the fairy crouched on her skin, slowly withdrawing her clawed fingers from Nelay's flesh. There was blood everywhere. Crying out, Nelay jerked her hand back.

The fairy toppled, rolling on the ground until she came to a jumbled stop and shook out her wings indignantly. Nelay snatched her spear and held it before her, but the fairy only cocked her head to the side.

Suddenly Nelay realized she was gripping her spear with her bitten hand. Refusing to let go of her spear, she inspected the wound. The puncture marks were still there, but the swelling and pain were gone.

She looked back at the blood on the ground. "I don't understand."

Siseth stood and brushed the dust from her scale dress. "I removed the venom. You will be fine. I cannot say the same for your father."

Nelay had completely forgotten him. She started running. By the time she reached him, she was out of breath and the world spun around her. She collapsed beside the thorny bush he lay under. "Father?"

There was no answer. His breathing had gone deep and heavy, the kind of heaviness that comes with death. "Father!" Nelay reached into the bush, ignoring the thorns hooking into her skin. She gripped him under the arms and pulled him free.

Nelay's hands fluttered over his body, but she didn't know where to touch him—how to help him.

"It is your father's time to die," Siseth said dispassionately, the beats of her wings smooth and even. "Even now, the shadows reach for him."

In the burning sun, Nelay felt cold. She thought of the baby her mother had perhaps given birth to by now. Her mother. Her brother. How would they survive the grief? "There must be something you can do."

"My price is steep."

Nelay thought she knew what the fairy was asking for—her mother had warned her that they were tricksy and cruel. But without Father to provide for them, they might all starve. "I'll die in his place."

The fairy's shivered. "Oh, that isn't my price, girl child."

Nelay worked her jaw. "Then what do you want?"

"I will come to you someday and ask for something. You will give it to me."

Nelay had heard stories of bargains made with fairies. "I won't give you my children."

"Children!" The fairy's wings trembled and Nelay realized she was laughing silently. "By the balance, what would I do with a human infant? No, I will ask some favor. And you will have no choice but to do it. Do you accept my bargain?"

Nelay glanced at her father's raw wound, his ashen face. Listened to the breathing of the dying. Grief scoured her from the inside out. Could even the fairy's magic save one so far gone? "Only if he lives."

The fairy made a sound of displeasure. "Clever, to ask for that." She fluttered over to the wounded leg, drew back her hand, and plunged in her claws. Nelay winced. As the fairy withdrew her claws, blood and viscous fluid oozed out, seeping into the starving ground.

The fairy flared her wings. "I don't have enough influence for the flower, but there are some favors I can call in. This will cost me, and therefore you."

Nelay didn't understand what Siseth meant. Before she could ask, the fairy flew away. "Wait," Nelay cried. "Where are you going? What flower?"

But the snake fairy was gone. Nelay touched her father's cold skin.

She heard a soft rustling and turned to see a fairy with shifting, rippling wings like turquoise water. The fairy ignored Nelay as she flitted over the ground and landed in a depression in the shade. She rested both hands on the ground. Curious, Nelay leaned forward.

The fairy collapsed suddenly, slumping over to the side. Nelay reached out to touch her—to help her, then hesitated. With her filmy dress and dewy skin, this fairy seemed so much more delicate than the snake fairy. Would the mere pressure of Nelay's fingers hurt her?

Thoughts of helping the fairy vanished as Nelay heard the gurgle of water. Her gaze locked on the depression the fairy had touched. Was it her imagination, or was the ground damp? Then Nelay saw the shine of water and lunged forward, prepared to dig it out before it could disappear. But there was already a puddle of water deep enough for her to sink her hands into. She lay flat on her stomach and sucked it up. The water was cold and clear and sweet. Her belly ached with the chill, and a dull nausea touched her.

Then she remembered her father and felt shame at not thinking of him first. She hauled the water skins over her head and dunked both into the water, the cold delicious against her hot, dry skin. She drank more while they filled.

When the last of the bubbles seeped from the water skins, she capped one and crawled to her father. She parted his cracked lips and poured a trickle of water into his mouth, but he didn't swallow. She felt her panic rising, cresting and threatening to drown her from the inside out, but then his throat worked. She poured more water into his mouth. Over the next hour, he drank two water skins, coming around enough to drink the last one mostly by himself, though he never opened his eyes.

Nelay went back to the pool. It was little more than damp earth now, and she had to dig to get more water, but she was used to that. She filled both water skins again and drank until she thought she would burst.

Then she turned back to the water fairy. The tiny creature's chest still rose and fell, but otherwise she hadn't moved. The snake fairy had transformed from a snake, so perhaps this fairy needed water.

As gently as she could, Nelay picked up the fairy. Her body filled most of Nelay's hand, and her wings were larger than they had appeared, cascading over Nelay's fingers and covering most of her wrist. They rippled like water and felt wet.

Nelay eased the fairy into the puddle. For a moment, nothing happened, and Nelay began to panic, but then the fairy shifted. After another moment, she moaned. Her eyes struggled open and she looked at Nelay and then at herself cupped in Nelay's hand. She closed her eyes, then opened them again and murmured something.

"What?" Nelay was mesmerized by the fairy's wings and hair, which flowed like a fountain.

"So that's why she helped you. What did you promise her?" Her voice flowed softly, but Nelay sensed it could turn to a torrent in a second.

"That I would give her a service."

The fairy's gaze turned inward. "Well, perhaps it's time things changed."

With a splash of water, she spread her wings and zipped away. Nelay watched her go, and when she turned back, it was as if she could still feel the weight of the fairy's body in her hands. And though the wings had felt wet, the places where they'd touched Nelay's wrists were dry.

Half smiling in wonder, Nelay turned to check on her father. Another fairy hovered over him, dragging a leaf over his raw wound. Nelay crawled to his side. The fairy had dark green wings and a sharp scent, like something herbal. She motioned to Nelay's pouch, the one she'd put the snake meat in earlier. "Open it."

Nelay held it open, and the fairy took hold of the flesh of her own arm and pulled. Her skin stretched away from her body in an oval shape about the size of a gourd seed. As Nelay gaped, the fairy dropped the seed into the pouch. The fairy pulled a seed from her other arm. Now the fairy seemed somehow smaller. After the fifth seed, Nelay was positive the fairy was shrinking. "How," she squeaked and had to clear her throat and try again. "How . . ." She couldn't manage to get more out.

The fairy looked at her curiously and then huffed. "It will grow back. All I have to do is rest in the soil with good sunlight and water."

Nelay nodded as if that made perfect sense.

The fairy flicked out her wings and took to the air. "Plant those in the shade where you live, and keep the soil moist. I'll make sure they grow. Take the leaves, bake them in oil, strain it three times, and pour the oil over his wound every day." She fluttered away without another word.

Seconds later, Asat came lumbering into view, a fairy with enormous ears and large, blocky teeth perched on the donkey's head. "She'll do whatever you ask now," said the fairy. "Get her something to drink. That water won't last." The fairy flew away.

Nelay hurried to the water hole and dug even deeper, so deep that the donkey had to crouch down on his knees to drink. And Nelay knew that was the last of the water.

She turned back to her father. He smelled of stringent herbs—like the shrinking fairy—but his color was better, his breathing lighter. Nelay wrapped his leg to keep the leaves on, knelt beside him, and shook his shoulder.

He opened bleary eyes and squinted up at her. "Nelay?" He glanced around as if looking for someone. "Did you get Benvi?"

It took her a moment to understand what he meant. He thought she'd already fetched their neighbor and come back for him. "No, Father. I found water and our donkey. I'm going to take you home."

He blinked at her in amazement. "I feel better—much better." He patted himself as if to make sure his words were true.

His words sang through her. Grinning, she braced herself behind him and pushed. "Come on, I need to get you back on Asat."

Her father sucked in a breath when he moved his leg. "Burns," he muttered.

With Nelay pushing, and him pulling, they finally managed to get him in onto the donkey's back. He promptly sprawled out over Asat's mane, but he seemed more aware this time.

Her muscles groaning in protest, Nelay led Asat across the valley, skirting the last few table mountains between her and home. The heat and light leached from the sky, leaving her with shadows as cold as day old ashes.

Shivering, she stumbled around rocks and bushes that reared in front of her in the dark. She stubbed her sandaled toe twice, but she was too tired to even curse under her breath. Four times, she had to backtrack to find another way through. Once, Asat ran into her back, sending her sprawling. For a moment, Nelay lay there, looking at the star-strewn sky and wanting nothing more than to close her eyes.

"Nelay?" her father said.

Tired to the bone, she pushed herself up, the grit on the ground scraping against her palms.

Just as the sky started to lighten, she saw lights. She was delirious with exhaustion. She couldn't get her tired mind to connect those lights with home, but she knew they meant help. She passed the scraggly wheat stalks that scratched at her robes. She wove through her family's grove of barren fruit trees, the branches creaking in the breeze. Then she plowed through the brittle herb garden, the smell of crushed spices releasing with each step.

Shivering with the cold, she stared at the wooden door that was bleached to a uniform gray with faded, cracked flowers carved into the surface. She wondered what to do. "Mother?" she finally called.

The door opened, and she saw her mother's shadowed face. "Nelay!" Her mother scooped Nelay's frozen body against her warm one, her enormous belly pressing hard against her.

"Father," Nelay managed. "He's on Asat."

Her mother put her down quickly and ran to the donkey's side. "Denar!"

"Mandana," came his weak reply.

Her mother cried out in relief as she half supported, half carried him into the house. She laid him down on their mud-brick platform covered with sheepskins. She unwrapped his foot as he groaned in pain, her face blanching at the sight of raw flesh. "Cursed snakes. Why hasn't the drought chased them away like everything else?"

Nelay was too exhausted to answer. She glanced around and realized someone was missing. "Panar?"

"He went for Benvi," her mother said as she went to the shelf on the wall.

Nelay remembered the seeds in her pouch—seeds made of fairy flesh. Carrying the pitcher of water they always kept on the table, she stumbled into the side yard next to the garden.

The seeds were small. Nelay knew to plant a seed twice as deep as it was long. She poured the water and pushed her finger into the mud, then dropped the seed inside the hole and pushed the sticky mud back over it. She put the pitcher down and sat back on her haunches, too tired to get back up and climb into the bed she shared with Panar.

That's when she saw Siseth watching her from the rocks around their well. When Nelay met her glinting gaze, the fairy smiled, showing her fangs and black mouth. Then she spread her wings and darted away.

Nelay watched her go, knowing she would one day pay dearly for the fairy's aid.

CHAPTER FIVE

Nelay woke to the door flying open. She sat up and saw Panar standing at the doorway, his black hair bathed in torchlight. "I brought Benvi!" he said.

Mother struggled up from the chair, her enormous abdomen preceding the rest of her. She gestured to the bed, where Father struggled to sit up. "Nelay brought him home."

As if he didn't believe her, Panar ran to the bed. "Father," he whispered. Then his gaze shifted to her. His nostrils flared and his eyes narrowed to slits. "But how? The donkey was gone."

Benvi stepped into the room, four of his sons behind him. "The child brought him home?"

All eyes turned to Nelay.

"I found water. Asat was there, drinking."

Benvi crossed the room in two of his giant strides. He stared at Father's raw foot. "It's not infected?" he said in disbelief.

His face a mask of tight control, Father uttered, "Not yet."

The two men clasped forearms. "What kind of snake?" Benvi asked.

"Black mamba," Father replied.

Benvi gasped. "But no one survives a bite from a mamba."

Father shook his head as if he didn't believe it himself. "I know."

41

All the adults exchanged glances, but Mother's gaze was fixed suspiciously on Nelay. Benvi ordered his sons to take the donkeys and go after the sheep—Panar was to show them where they were. No one had any illusions about the animals surviving, but their hides would probably be salvageable.

Tears choking her, Nelay slipped out while they were still arranging everything. She stumbled to a halt when she noticed the seeds she'd planted last night were ready for harvesting. She dropped to her knees as if her legs had been cut out from under her. Hesitantly, she reached out to touch the puffy flowers, touching their feather-soft tips with her fingers.

Her mother stood beside her, breathing hard. "I don't remember these being here. Must be some sort of weed."

Nelay didn't answer as she dug her nail into the base of the leaves and snapped them off. "If you bake them with oil, it helps keep the rot out of the wound."

Her mother fanned her red face with her headscarf. "How do you know that?"

Nelay forced herself to meet her mother's gaze. "Nanu told me." Nanu was Benvi's wife.

"You didn't learn it from *them*, did you?" Mother's voice was strained.

"No. I promise I didn't."

Grimacing in pain, her mother massaged her stomach. "You remember what I've always taught you?"

Nelay couldn't meet her mother's gaze and was glad she seemed distracted. "When men and goddesses mix, men always lose," Nelay repeated. But wasn't her father alive because she had approached the fairies?

She tentatively reached out and placed the leaves in her mother's hand. "How do we lose?"

Her mother closed her eyes as if counting. After a long time, she answered, "If they use their power contrary to its purpose, they go against nature, upsetting the balance. In order to

OF FIRE AND ASH

right itself, the balance takes it back. So if they grant you rain one year, the balance will give you a drought the next. If a fairy heals your fig tree, your pomegranate will die."

Nelay's mouth felt so dry. She was on the verge of asking her mother what the balance would take for sparing her father, but her mother groaned, her eyes closed again. Something was wrong—terribly wrong.

"Mother? What is it?"

Her mother's normally dark skin was pale. She pushed herself clumsily to her feet and staggered toward the door. Nelay jumped up to help her, and only then did she notice the bright red blood where her mother had been sitting, and the shining drops trailing her every step.

Benvi's youngest son was sent back to his house with Nelay's father on the back of a donkey and implicit instructions to fetch his mother and older sisters. Meanwhile Panar, Benvi, and the rest of his sons set out with the remaining donkeys and leather water skins to see if they could find the family's sheep.

All through the day, Nelay's mother labored. When night came, Nelay lay wrapped in sheepskins on top of the courtyard wall—for there she was safe from snakes—her gaze trained on the stars as her mother's groans progressed to cries and then to screams.

Nelay pressed her sheepskin fur against her ears, but could still hear her mother's pain rise to a crescendo. And then everything was hushed and quiet.

Nelay held her breath, waiting. But there was no sound of a baby crying.

Unable to bear it, she got up, the cold air harsh against her skin. She paused at the doorway, then inched up the lever and pushed the door open.

43

Her mother lay naked on the sheepskins, her abdomen mushy-looking and her breasts hard. She had turned her face to the wall, and silent sobs wracked her body. One of the women had wrapped the baby in a tight bundle and set it on the table.

Dread tore through Nelay and she slipped inside the house, unnoticed by the women. She picked up the tiny baby and gently unwrapped it to reveal a perfectly formed face. He was much larger than Mother's previous babies, and quite handsome. And unnaturally blue. He was dead.

As the inconsequential weight settled in Nelay's hands, a terrible knowing burned through her. She had traded this life for her father's.

"Nelay?" Her head jerked up. Nanu came toward her, arms outstretched. "He was born dead. I'm sorry."

Nelay looked past her to see her mother watching her. At the grief in that gaze, Nelay's guilt flared up hot. She shoved her dead brother into Nanu's arms and ran into the night, her mother's high pitched keening following her. She didn't know where to go, and even as young as she was, she knew the dangers of running unseeing through the desert. So she climbed the shade tree in their courtyard, going high up in the branches. And there she stayed as dawn came, bright and hard and indifferent to Nelay's broken heart.

With the sun came the men with Panar. On the donkey's backs were the fresh skins of her family's sheep. She recognized Mag's black-and-white wool. The skin with the mangled ear was Day. And the one with the dirty ring around the wool of her neck where a collar and bell had once been, that was Blua's.

Tears blurred Nelay's vision. Those animals had trusted her to take care of them. She had cursed them more times than not, but she had loved them all the same. And now they were dead. As her baby brother was. And it was Nelay's fault.

Panar dropped down from the donkey as Nanu slipped outside. Before he could react, she enveloped him in a hug, as she had probably meant to do with Nelay before she darted out last night, and whispered in his ear. From her perch on a wide branch, Nelay watched as Panar shrugged Nanu off and cast an embarrassed look back at the men before walking away to help them unload the sheepskins.

Nelay's mouth tightened. How could he care more about what the men thought of him than of their mother's grief? He handled the sheepskins as if they were nothing more than blankets as they tacked them up to be scraped. Nelay felt her gorge rising and had to look away.

Not long after they arrived, her father came from Benvi's house, hope bright on his face. Once again, Nelay turned away, her gaze catching on a fairy watching her with her head cocked to the side. Nelay stared into the fairy's golden eyes. The wings at her back matched the long, thin leaves rustling with the breeze.

Nelay heard Benvi knock softly on the door. A few murmured words passed, and then the door shut softly.

Benvi didn't mince words. "Your son is dead, Denar. Your wife lives, but she is very weak."

Tears brimmed in Nelay's swollen eyes and dropped onto the bark of the tree. The fairy flew forward and touched one, her brow creased in confusion. She fluttered closer to Nelay, catching one of the drops as it rolled down her cheek. She held it in her splinter-like fingers, sniffing it, and then her paper tongue flicked out to taste it. She jerked back and shook her head. "Ugh, that's nothing like sap." She studied Nelay. "But it is some kind of wound, all the same." She took a deep breath. "But I am a willow fairy. I know not how to heal it." She flew slowly away, touching the tree in places, but her gaze kept straying to Nelay.

"Burn him and bury the ashes beside the others."

Nelay's father's head hung low.

There were seven scorch marks in their backyard. And not all of the babies had died at birth. Nelay had memories of many of them. Gummy smiles and fat fingers in her hand. Bruised foreheads and jabbering voices.

Benvi set his sons about fixing up a bed for her father in the shade of the tree where Nelay perched. Lying on her stomach over the branch, she watched the women bring him tea and baked bean cakes.

The smell filtered through the branches, and Nelay's stomach growled, but she fiercely ignored it as wood was gathered. They laid the tiny body on the top of the stack and lit the wood. Nelay's mother didn't come out, though most of the women did.

Nelay forced herself not to look away. As the flames spread across her brother's body, they spread through her heart, burning away her tears and leaving her feeling like weeks-old ashes that the merest wind might blow away. Once the fire turned to embers, the ashes were scattered.

When it was finished, Benvi set his sons who weren't scraping hides to doing the chores while he sat beside her father. "Denar, I am sorry for your loss. I will help you in whatever way I can."

Father stared at his hands as if wondering how they could still be connected to his body. "What can you do, Benvi? You, who have more mouths to feed than I."

Benvi drew his knees into his chest. "But we have had better luck than you, my friend. Perhaps it's time we shared that luck. My oldest is in need of a wife."

Nelay's mouth fell open and she looked at Haddi, who was caring for their goats. He had a full beard, and thick brows that protruded over his eyes.

"Haddi is near twenty-five," Father said.

Nelay recoiled. Even though such marriage arrangements were not uncommon in Idara, she had never considered that such an arrangement might be made for her. And Haddi was practically an old man!

Benvi nodded. "This is true. And Nelay is only nine. But she will be of child-bearing age in five years. I will take her into my household as a daughter and raise her up. When she comes of age, Haddi will be well established and able to care for a wife and their children. I will give you eight sheep for her."

It shocked Nelay when her father didn't immediately say no, that he seemed to be considering it. "I don't think she would be happy about leaving," he finally said.

"She's too young to understand such things," Benvi reasoned. "Simply tell her that we are caring for her until your family has enough food for everyone."

With a sigh, her father tipped his face up. His gaze snagged on Nelay's, and a single brow rose in surprise. "I'm afraid it is too late for that. Come down, Nelay."

She climbed carefully down, aware of her father and Benvi watching her every move. She stepped to the ground and turned her back to them, her arms crossed over her chest.

"What say you, Daughter?" her father said gently.

Nelay's voice came out in a squeak. "I want to stay here."

Father nodded. "I'm not sure how I will feed you. Would you not rather go with Benvi, to be treated as one of his daughters, and when you are ready, marry his son, whom I know to be a good and obedient man?"

Nelay thought she would choke on the knot in her throat. Maybe she deserved this. Maybe it was the price she must pay for breaking her mother's rules. But she couldn't bring herself to do the unselfish thing and say yes.

When she didn't answer, her father sighed. "We can give her time. I cannot care for even one sheep at present, let alone eight. Your boys have slaughtered the sheep—their meat will last us a long time. I do not think Nelay's mother would part with her either, not with such a recent loss in her heart. If your offer will last that long?"

"It will last as long as you need it, Denar. If Haddi finds another before that time comes, there is no reason the next oldest cannot take Nelay to wife."

Father tapped his forehead in respect. "You are a good man and a good friend."

Benvi nodded. "I would consider it an honor to have a child of your house join with mine." He rose, inclining his head. "Send Panar if you need anything. We'll take care of the hides at our home."

"Thank you," Father responded.

Benvi sighed. "I only wish I could offer more."

He departed, taking their hides with him, and Nelay was left shaking at the thought of losing her family.

Her father looked at her. "I know you do not want this, Daughter. And I will not force you. Perhaps we can find another way."

Nelay couldn't answer him. She stumbled off into the heat of the ovat. She climbed the nearest table mountain and scaled a large collection of rocks shaped like a rabbit's head. She perched on what would be his nose and looked out over the barren landscape.

She didn't know how long she sat in the shade of the rocks before she finally looked down. She was shocked to find Siseth sitting directly in front of her, mimicking her position, down to her hugged knees. With her wings tucked against her body, the fairy looked much less threatening.

Tears sprang to Nelay's eyes. "Why didn't you warn me?"

The fairy watched her with a narrowed gaze. "Would it have changed anything?"

Nelay sniffed. "I don't know." If she hadn't made the deal, her father would have died. She wiped her nose with the back of her sleeve. "I'm the one who made the bargain. I should have died instead."

The fairy actually looked sad. "You are much too hard to kill for the balance to bother with you."

Nelay half shook her head. "What does that mean?"

The fairy fanned her wings behind her. "It means you weren't the only one to make a deal with the fairies."

Nelay's eyes widened. "What?"

The fairy spread her wings and tipped back, pushing off the rock and letting an air current hold her aloft. "Ask your mother."

Nelay's breath caught in her throat. "What do you mean?"

The fairy flew away.

"And my promise? Will it cost too much?" Nelay called after her.

"It always does," the fairy responded without looking back.

CHAPTER SIX

Nelay climbed to the highest branch she dared and stretched out, reaching for the date. It was still too far. Holding the fruit she'd already gathered in her apron, she slid her foot forward a fraction and stretched out, but her fingers only pushed the date farther away. Then the branch cracked and she slipped, tearing her way through branches and leaves that scratched at her. She landed on her bottom and yelped while sucking in a breath.

The fruit she'd already picked pelted her so she covered her head. Then she glanced up, glaring at the stupid tree as if it had done it on purpose. Her vision suddenly went red and she blinked and rubbed at it. Her fingers came away wet with blood. She gingerly probed her face until she found a shallow cut in the middle of her eyebrow. After she'd mopped up the blood with the corner of her robe, she rolled to her knees and started gathering the dates back into a basket.

She only got about halfway when she heard someone coming. She glanced up to see her brother striding through the grove, his sling in hand. He veered toward her when he saw her, surveying her with a condescending tilt of his head.

"Not so perfect now, are you?"

Panar had been unbearable in the three weeks since Nelay had saved their father. The day when everything had changed.

Nelay waited for her parents to laugh, for her mother to touch her with her gentle hands, for her father to whittle, wood shavings surrounding his chair. But there was only silence—silence with a weight and a suffocating presence that drove Nelay from the house more and more often. She spent her time in their grove, watering the trees, which had almost stopped producing altogether. She tended the gardens and the scraggly field of wheat. And despite the back-breaking work, the crops were still sparse.

"I never said I was perfect," she said to her brother, then gathered the last of the dates and pushed to her feet. She tried to go around him, but he moved to block her.

"How did you magically find that water, Nelay? It wasn't there before."

Nelay's jaw tightened until it ached. She considered telling him—what harm would it do now? But she didn't trust him, and she didn't want to share something so big with him, something he could use to hurt her later. "Perhaps the goddess took pity on us."

Panar snorted. "Liar."

Nelay let out all of her breath. She was tired of fighting and of silence. "Just leave me alone." She tried to push past him, but he shoved her to the ground, where she landed on her sore backside.

She sucked in a sharp breath as he bent down. "You always have to be the best. Perfect Nelay." His words were hot against her cheek.

She kept the pain from showing on her face. "I won't pretend to be stupid so you can feel wise."

He raised his hand. Nelay's gaze hardened. "I'll tell Father."

It didn't stop Panar from punching her in the stomach. All the air left her in a *whoosh* and then he was gone, running out of the grove.

Nelay tried to stop the tears, but the more she tried, the faster they came. She grabbed the basket of small dates and stumbled back to the house, where she collapsed in her father's arms and told him what Panar had done to her when she'd killed the snake. What he'd done to her just now.

When she finished and the front of father's shirt was wet, she pulled back to look at him. His eyes were shadowed and sunken from pain and poor health. His foot was healing, albeit slowly. The pain kept him from sleeping more than a few fitful snatches in the day. "Daughter, Panar would not do such a thing."

She showed him her stomach, which was still red. Father's mouth tightened. "I'll speak with him when he comes home."

Sniffing, she nodded.

He rested his heavy hands on her shoulders. "Have you seen your mother outside?" Nelay shook her head. "Why don't you go find her and take her some of those dates? I don't think she ate anything this morning."

Nelay hesitated. "I will if you carve something."

Her father drew in a long breath and let it out slowly. "All right."

Feeling a bit better, Nelay stepped back into the late morning light. She'd just come from the grove, so she checked the outbuilding and the shed. She wandered past the field and garden. She'd almost given up when she finally checked the grove.

Her mother lay beneath the tree amid the ashes of her children. Close enough to hear Panar and Nelay fighting. And she'd done nothing to stop it.

Hurt built inside Nelay until she thought it would burst out of her like a boil. She hesitated, scratching the back of her leg with the opposite foot's toenail. But looking at her mother's empty face, pity replaced the anger. So much heartache, bringing children into the world. And Nelay's father wanted to marry her off to a man more than twice her age and condemn her to a similar life.

She remembered what Panar had said—that he would be someone important while she would be forced to be a pregnant wife. She swore then that she would never have children. Never marry a man, if that's what it took.

Steeling herself, Nelay knelt before her mother and set the basket in front of her. But her mother didn't even acknowledge her presence.

"Mother," she said hesitantly. "I've brought you something to eat." Still nothing. "Please. You need to eat."

Nelay reached down and rested a hand on her shoulder to shake her slightly. Only then did she see that the front of her mother's shirt was crusted with dried milk that had leaked from her breasts. This close, Nelay could smell her mother's unwashed body and rotten milk.

She sat back on her haunches. Her mother had hardly eaten since the baby's birth. Her skin hung limp over her bones. She rarely got up longer than was necessary to relieve her bladder and then lie back down. Looking at her, suspicion grew in Nelay's breast. Her mother wanted to die. Was waiting for it.

Nelay pushed the basket closer. "Please, Mother, you must eat."

Her mother stared at the food as if it was something foreign and incomprehensible. Then she went back to staring at nothing.

Nelay bowed her head. "Would you like me to bring you water for washing?" When her mother didn't answer, Nelay decided that was as good as a yes. She drew water from the well and fetched their soap. Back at the grove, she tried to get her mother to stand up. Tried to get her clothes off. In the end, all she managed was to get her sitting on a flat rock.

Nelay poured half the bucket on her mother, who barely seemed to notice. Nelay scrubbed her, clothes and all, as best she could manage, which wasn't very good, but her mother did smell better.

Then she poured the other half of the bucket over her mother to rinse her off. When Nelay finished, her mother still stared off into nothing as if something inside her had broken. With a fair amount of coaxing and some physical force, Nelay finally managed to get her into the house, where she slumped down, still sopping wet, onto her bed.

Her father watched from where he'd taken up residence by the doorway, his carving knife in one hand and a lump of wood in the other. His other leg was propped up on a stool. Curls of wood fell to the floor, and the air smelled of resin.

"Will she be all right?" Nelay asked him.

"It's always hard for her." He seemed to have difficulty swallowing. "But she eventually comes out of it."

Nelay nodded, then went back out and began hauling bucket after bucket up from the well to water the trees. At midday, the beginning of the ovat sent her toward the house. She was eager for smoked sheep meat—they might have been her friends, but for the first time in months she hadn't gone hungry—and an afternoon nap.

But she paused at the sight of a cloud of dust beyond the trees and bushes that hid their house. She could hear the sound of many feet. A herd? A large one by the sound of it. As she watched, a strange shape appeared over the rise. This was not a herd of sheep or shaggy donkeys Nelay was used to, but a caravan of camels—something only the very rich could afford. There were five of them. The first had a shade pavilion to protect its rider. The rest of the camels seemed to be loaded down with supplies.

The only person Nelay knew who owned camels was the provincial lord. "Father?" she called, squinting for a better look. Usually, some of the lord's men would come for taxes on the land. "Is the lord coming?"

Her father looked up from the front of their house, where he'd started carving himself a cane. He pulled himself up and limped painfully forward, the partially carved cane tapping.

And then foot soldiers came into view. Her father frowned. "That's not the lord."

Nelay backed away. "Then who are they?"

He whistled loudly for Panar, who hadn't showed up since he'd punched Nelay and was probably beyond hearing. Her father hobbled into the house and pushed aside his sheepskin bedding to reveal a loose bit of mud brick at the base of his bed. He pulled it free, reached in, and came out with the curving sword that had belonged to Nelay's grandfather. It was nicked and tarnished, but still the most beautifully crafted thing she had ever seen.

And all the while, her mother still hadn't moved.

Suddenly afraid, Nelay snatched her sling and stones and filled the cup.

"Stay with your mother," Father said as he pushed Nelay behind him.

"But Father!" She held out her sling to remind him what a good shot she was.

He limped to the door, grimacing with each step. "If they get past me, you're better off begging for mercy than angering them."

Nelay wanted to point out that he could barely walk and his free hand had to hold the cane, but fear kept her quiet. She took her mother's limp hand and squeezed.

Her father stepped in front of the doorway, his sword out of sight behind the frame. Nelay peeked past him to watch as the camels came into the yard with a glide that ended in a lurch. The creatures were resplendent, with beautiful red trappings trimmed out with gold tassels, patterns of flames throughout.

Surrounding the five camels were dozens of foot soldiers in black, their headscarves pulled over their faces so only their eyes showed. They wore robes that ended at their shins, with fitted pants and quiet boots.

They flooded into the yard, paying Nelay's family no mind as they spread out and crept through the shadows of the sparse grove and fields as if searching for danger.

A foot soldier with a glittering gold medallion in the center of his headscarf spoke to the first camel and slapped the creature's shoulder. It lowered jerkily to the ground. Atop the camel was a woman who wore a headdress over thick black hair and a long, sheer veil over her mouth. As she stepped down, Nelay stared at her bell-shaped pants and the fitted bodice that showed her stomach. Her eyes were lined with kohl. Even with the dust of travel, her clothing shone with colors and jewels that made Nelay's ragged, sun-bleached garments seem like a moth in a field of butterflies.

"I am Suka, high priestess to the Goddess of Fire," the woman declared.

Her mother stirred, but Nelay hardly noticed. High priestess—that was impossible. The high priestess lived in the temple at Thanjavar. But her clothes . . . the jewels, the camels. It must be true.

As if Nelay's father had come to the same conclusion, the sword fell from his fingers, clanging on the floor. The woman raised a single eyebrow, and her guards stepped protectively closer.

Nelay remembered what her mother always said—that if Nelay revealed her secret, the priestesses would take her away. And she knew they were here for her.

When her father still said nothing, the woman let out a long sigh. "Have my men the use of the well to water our camels?"

Nelay's father finally found his voice. "Y-yes. Of course." He bowed low. "May the fire ever burn within you."

The woman inclined her head. "And with you."

Nelay's mother sat up, looking confused. Nelay stepped closer. "Mother, the priestess is here."

Her father looked back at them before wetting his lips and turning back to Suka. "What cause has a Priestess of Fire to come here?"

The woman moved closer, her eyes slipping past Nelay's father to land on her. Outwardly, she was all poise, but Nelay caught a hungry flash in her gaze. "May I come in?" the priestess asked. "The ovat is upon us, and I am in need of a place to rest."

Nelay's mother had pushed herself up on her arms, and though her gaze was still hazy, it was no longer empty. "No." Her voice sounded rusty and disused.

Nelay's mouth dropped open. This woman served the Goddess of Fire. Her rank equaled the king's. And Nelay's mother was defying her.

Suka's gaze traveled from Mandana's matted hair stuck to the side of her face, over her battered robes, which were still damp in places, to her dirty bare feet.

"Of course you may rest inside." Father shot Mother a glare that was half pleading as he stepped out of the doorway.

The woman came inside, unfastening her veil to reveal delicate tattoos where the hair had been shaved above her ears. The tattoos spread in curling-fire filigree, framing her face.

High Priestess Suka filled up the room in ways the four members of Nelay's family never had. She looked down at Nelay, her smile gentle, but Nelay couldn't forget the hunger she'd seen earlier. "Child, my maidservant is without—go and fetch refreshments from her."

Nelay looked to her father to see what to do.

"Don't let her go," her mother said to her father.

When he hesitated, Suka only smiled. "We will not steal her away from you, Denar."

57

Nelay's mouth fell open. How did Suka know her father's name? Her father stiffened, but he nodded for Nelay to do as the high priestess had asked.

She stepped out and approached the camels warily. She hadn't had any dealings with camels, and they were so large and strange looking they made her nervous. But they paid her no mind, drinking buckets full of water as if they were thimbles.

A woman wearing fine orange bell-shaped pants, a fitted sleeveless bodice, and a swath of fabric draped around her took her time unpacking provisions from one of the camel's backs.

Nelay eased slowly forward, and the woman finally set the food neatly in a basket and handed it to Nelay without meeting her gaze. She took the basket full of more food than one woman could possibly eat and turned back to the house. Resting one side of the basket between her hip and the frame, Nelay used her other hand to push the door open.

What she saw stopped her cold. Dozens of silver coins sat on the table, more money than her family would see in three lifetimes. And even more shocking, her mother was out of the bed, sitting at the table, her gaze fierce and angry. "No. I won't lose another child. I won't."

Lose another child? It took Nelay a moment to realize they meant her.

"And this is worse than giving her to Benvi?" Father stared at mother, his gaze soft.

"At least if she goes to Benvi, I'll see her again. I'll be able to play with my grandchildren. If she goes with these priestesses, we'll lose her forever!"

"That is not true, Mandana. If you come to Thanjavar, you will be permitted to see her," Suka said soothingly.

"But she will no longer be my daughter! She will be yours!" Mother lurched up unsteadily from the table. "And when will I ever be able to make such a journey? A woman cannot travel alone, and my husband will never be able to leave his sheep."

She started when she saw Nelay watching them from the doorway.

All their eyes fell on her.

Mother turned away, but Nelay could still hear the tears in her voice. "The answer is no."

Suka sighed. "I thank you for your answer, Mandana, but I would hear from your husband and the girl as well." She gestured for Father to speak.

He took a deep breath, but instead of speaking to Suka, he gestured for Nelay to come closer. Leaning toward her, he took both her hands in his. "Daughter, do you understand who this woman is?"

Nelay swallowed. "A priestess from the Temple of Fire."

Father nodded. "Yes, child. And she says you are to come with her as one of their acolytes."

Nelay shot the woman a glance, but she didn't dare hold her hungry gaze. She felt shabby and drab and small next to her.

"Their temple is in Thanjavar, two weeks' journey away," her father went on.

"What should I do, Father?"

He looked up at the ceiling and then back at her. "If you stay here, you will have to go to Benvi and live with his family. When you are fourteen, you will be married to Hanni. Benvi will give us enough sheep to start over. And when I am old, Panar will take over this place and raise children of his own. If you go with these women . . ." Nelay's father's words trailed off.

Suka leaned forward. "You will be trained to fight. Trained to administer the rites and perform the ceremonies. We will be your family, and the fruits of your labors will be as your children. And as you obey your mother and father, you must obey the priestesses."

"Would you come see me?" Nelay asked her father.

His gaze went to Suka. "She has promised that if we go to Thanjavar, they will allow us to see you."

"But Mother said you wouldn't be able to leave the sheep," Nelay said softly.

He hesitated. "When Panar is old enough to care for them himself, we will come."

Nelay looked out the door, at the row of graves, the babies her mother had buried. The empty look in her mother's eyes. The weight of her youngest brother's death and her guilt over her lies and silence seemed to take more from her every day. And she remembered her promise to never have children. "I'll go with them."

Her mother gave a small cry and ran from the room, disappearing into the burning heat. Nelay turned and went after her. She found her at the graves, kneeling next to the rock Nelay had bathed her on. "Mother?" she said softly.

"You lied to me—you said you hadn't spoken to them." Her mother slowed her rocking. "Am I to lose all my children?"

Nelay closed her eyes. "I lied to you. I asked Siseth to help me. And she did. Father lived. And the baby died." Nelay pressed her hand to her chest—it was like she was burning from the inside out, and each day a little more of her turned to ash. "It's my fault."

Her mother's answer came in a whisper. "I spoke to them once."

Nelay gaped at her. "What?"

Her mother closed her eyes, tears leaking from her lids. "I lost five babies before you were born. They were so tiny they fit in the palm of my hand. Each one was perfect. Each one was dead."

Nelay hadn't known her mother had miscarried so many babies. All she remembered were the ones who came after her, the ones who had either been born dead or died in their first few years.

A breath shuddered through her mother's body like wind through an empty building. "And then you came. You were perfect and strong. And then you weren't. I watched as you wasted away to a skeleton-thin baby. You were dying.

"I found one of them and asked for help. She brought me a single white petal and told me to put it in your mouth.

"You were never sick again—not so much as a stuffy nose."

Nelay let out a long breath. "Who died?"

Her mother's gaze finally landed on Nelay's. "Whoever is most vulnerable and close. In this case, my mother." She shuddered.

A single tear rolled down Nelay's cheek. "It's my fault—him dying."

Her mother raised haunted eyes. "No. It's mine. I should have told you exactly what would happen."

Nelay knelt next to her mother. "But you warned me never to speak to them. Never to let them know I could see them. That in a deal with them, they always win. That should have been enough."

Her mother wiped Nelay's cheek with the back of her hand. "You still would have saved him—he's your father." Her mother let out a sigh. "These burdens are too heavy for one so young. Shrug them off, Daughter."

"Can you forgive me?" Nelay whispered.

"There's nothing to forgive. You did the best you could. You saved your father's life. We would be destitute without him. I would have had to marry someone, quickly, in order to provide for you, your brother, and the baby." She seemed to be trying to convince herself instead of Nelay.

"So you see, you can stay," her mother went on. "I'll get better, I know I will. And you will forgive yourself. Someday, you will marry Haddi and bring your own children into this world."

Nelay wrapped her arms around herself. "I don't want that, Mother."

Her mother's wet eyes opened wider. "What?"

"Marrying Haddi—that feels like dying inside."

"Well, there are other sons—"

Nelay gestured to the ashes still blowing around the trees. "I don't want a baby." She had seen them tear apart her mother's body, and then most of them ended up in the ground. A wash of shame covered her from head to toe. "I want to go with the priestesses."

Her mother squeezed a handful of dirt.

"But I don't want to hurt you," Nelay said softly.

"Go," her mother said tightly. "I see that you must. But know that you take my heart with you."

She looked past Nelay and spoke again. "I leave off bearing. No more children shall I bring forth for you, Denar."

Nelay turned to see her father standing behind her, his eyes wet with compassion, and Nelay realized he'd heard her. He knew what she'd done.

He also knew his wife and daughter had the sight. "Mandana," he whispered. "Is this why they have come for her? Could they somehow know she spoke to the fairies?"

Or did they somehow know that her mother had changed her as a baby, Nelay wondered.

Without answering, Mother stumbled past them and staggered away, loose dirt falling from her hands. Nelay's father's throat worked as if he was trying to swallow something that simply wouldn't fit.

"Father," Nelay said softly. "Is Mother broken?"

"Yes, but she will fix herself. She just needs time."

"Am I breaking her?"

He shook his head. "They will teach you to read and write. You will be a woman of power." His voice was choked with emotion. "And you will never go hungry again. That's not something you can turn away from, Daughter."

"But what about Mother?" Tears fell fast down Nelay's cheeks.

Father looked down at her. "Your brother and I will look after her."

"But—"

He crouched down in front of her. "Nelay, if you do not go, we will have to send you to Benvi—otherwise we will all starve. Which would you choose?"

"The priestesses," she said in a whisper.

He rose and held out his hand. "Come. High Priestess Suka has laid out food in celebration."

The table was laden with food, more even than Nelay had carried in the first time. There were dried figs baked in cakes with pecans, exotic cheese, and salted crackers.

Suka gestured for them to join her. Nelay perched on the edge of her chair. Suka lifted a glass pendant from around her neck. She spoke a prayer in ancient Idaran, but Nelay only understanding a portion of it. Then Suka smiled at them, her gaze lingering on Nelay.

Though Nelay's stomach knotted inside her, she couldn't help but try each dish. She'd never eaten food so rich, and judging by the way Suka picked at her meal, this was all very simple fare for the priestess.

Halfway through, there was a commotion outside. Moments later, Panar stood at the doorway, one of the foot soldiers holding his arm. "I assume this is another of your children?" the soldier asked blandly. "He was trying to sneak in."

"Yes," Nelay's father said quickly, rising from the table.

"Don't trouble yourself, Denar," Suka said. "The boy can join us. There's more than any of us could ever eat."

Panar's gaze flitted across all of them. A blush burned across his cheeks when he looked at Suka. He shuffled forward, keeping his head down as he plopped onto another chair.

Suka reached out and brushed her fingers along the top of his hand. "No need to be shy. Take what you like. It's a gift."

Panar finally looked up, his gaze taking in Suka's finery with a touch of adoration. "What . . ." His voice broke, and he cleared his throat and spoke deeper than normal, as if trying to impress her. "Why are you here?"

Suka smiled, her eyes laughing at Panar, but he didn't seem to notice. "Your sister is going to come with us, to become one of our priestesses."

Panar stiffened as if his spine had suddenly fused. He turned slowly to look at Nelay, jealousy hot in his gaze.

Turning her head so her father and Suka wouldn't see, Nelay shot Panar a smug smile—simply to hurt him. His nostrils flared and he looked like he might explode.

"Panar, try some of the food," Father said sharply.

Panar reached out and snatched a handful of candied nuts, then shoved them into his mouth in a way that made Nelay cringe inside, though it hadn't bothered her at breakfast. "Where's Mother?" he asked.

Father gave a helpless shrug.

"I'm going to find her," Panar said.

As he stood up to leave, Father called out to him, "Kiss your sister goodbye."

Panar turned back to Nelay, his expression hard. She tried to move away as he leaned forward. But he didn't touch her, just whispered in her ear, "I'm glad you're going. Glad I'll never have to see you again."

He spun around and left without looking back.

Nelay didn't want to admit it, but his words stung. She wanted her brother to love her, even if she wished she didn't.

They finished eating, but the food tasted like ash in Nelay's mouth. Then they settled down to rest for the duration of the ovat. The high priestess took Nelay's father's bed, even though he was injured and she was not. He and Nelay shared her bed, but Nelay didn't sleep. Too many emotions swirled inside her.

When the ovat ended, the high priestess glided outside. She stepped back onto the camel and waited.

Nelay's hand felt very small inside her father's. "Will . . . will you be all right?" she asked, her voice small. But what she really meant was, can you forgive me for what I've done? For what I am doing?

Father knelt in front of her. He swallowed once, twice. "I'm sorry, Daughter, that it has come to this."

She gave a small shrug. "I'm the only thing of value you have left."

He gripped her to him. "Would that it were not so."

He so rarely held her that the contact brought tears to her eyes. "Mother—is she not going to say goodbye?"

Her father held her back to eye level. "I—"

"I'm right here," Mother said as she came around from the other side of the house.

Nelay flew into her arms and felt the flesh and bones of her body, soft and fragile where Nelay's was wiry and hard. Her mother held her, and they both sobbed.

"Make us proud, Daughter," her mother finally whispered.

"I will."

Her mother kissed both cheeks, holding her face between her hands as if to memorize each detail, each curve and hollow.

Her father took hold of Nelay's middle and passed her into Suka's waiting arms.

As the camel pitched clumsily to its feet, Nelay watched her mother bury her face in her father's chest. Watched Panar glare at her from behind their parents, his eyes full of hate. Watched as all that she had ever known disappeared.

And then she turned toward what lay ahead—a future very different from what she had ever imagined. But somewhere beyond the sadness, excitement stirred. If she was to be a priestess, by the goddess, she would be the best priestess ever born.

Amber Argyle is the number-one bestselling author of the Witch Song Series and the Fairy Queen Series. Her books have been nominated for and won awards and have been translated into French and Indonesian.

Amber graduated cum laude from Utah State University with a degree in English and physical education, a husband, and a two-year-old. Since then, she and her husband have added two more children, which they are actively trying to transform from crazy small people into less crazy larger people.

Visit Amber Argyle's website to sign up for her free starter library or to learn more: amberargyle.com

OTHER TITLES BY AMBER ARGYLE

CPSIA information can be obtained
at www.ICGtesting.com
Printed in the USA
LVOW13s0523040717

540203LV00035B/1424/P

9 780997 639001